Unicorn Stories

The Unicorn and the Little Goldfish

Jan Rylewicz

Om KIDZ

An imprint of Om Books International

It was too crowded in the water. Wherever Bubbles, the goldfish swam, he bumped into someone.
On his way to the fish school, he bumped into Blubber, the blue whale.
At night, the whales snored loudly above his waterbed.
He tossed and turned.
"How am I ever supposed to sleep like this?" he wondered.

The next night, Bubbles watched the bright moonlight dance above him.
He shyly poked his head out of the water.
He saw a beautiful winged horse drinking from the pond. She was covered in moonlight.
"Are you really a unicorn?" Bubbles asked.
She lifted her head, and nodded.
"Yes, I am Reema, the unicorn. I like your pretty colour. You must be a goldfish."

“It is so crowded down here,” moaned Bubbles. Reema explained that it was her fault. She wanted all the fish to get along. That’s why she made even the sharks, vegetarian.

“What does that mean?” asked Bubbles.

“It means that they do not eat other fish, but it also means your pond is over-crowded,” explained Reema.

The next morning, Bubbles met his friend Stormy, the shark. He didn't tell him about meeting Reema.

"Are you a vegetarian?" he asked.

"I wish I weren't," said Stormy and flashed his bright gold tooth.

"Why?" asked Bubbles.

"Because then I could eat goldfish again,"grinned his friend.

From now on, Reema and Bubbles met regularly.
Together they came up with a fantastic plan to make life better for all the fish and shells in the pond!

It was the weekend and there was no school for Bubbles and his friends. The sun shone in the blue sky.

Reema put up a sign next to the water which read:
'MOUNTAIN PLEASURE FLIGHTS.'
The plan was to take all the fish up into the air and fly them around the mountain. Up in the air the fish could forget all about being trapped in the pond.

Brave Bubbles went up first. The flight on the unicorn was an amazing experience. No goldfish had ever made it this far up in the world!

"Most goldfish have never left their aquariums. I am so lucky!" he said.
Only Stormy, the shark, looked angry. He was too scared to fly, and even the weaker fish laughed at him! "You all wait and see!" hissed Stormy gnashing his teeth.

Bubbles flew safely inside a large water bubble on Reema's back. They flew past a family of geese. He waved at them with his fins.
"Yoo-Hoo!" he shouted, smiling.
The geese looked very surprised.
He spotted bear cubs dancing around in the snow on the mountain.
He saw Yeti, the great mountain monster.
Even the Yeti waved at him!

Many other fish flew high on Reema's back that day. They saw men and women in the market, tiny as peas. They flew through the clouds which were very cold inside. Walter, the walrus, waved at an airplane in the sky.

"Look, mummy, a flying walrus!" said a small girl inside the plane.

"Don't be silly," answered her mother.

Long after the weekend of Reema's Pleasure Flights, every fish in the pond still talked about it.

The beautiful unicorn made them feel so special. They hoped that she would come back.
But Bubbles began to forget about her. As a goldfish, his memory was very poor.

He forgot all about flying, the geese and the Yeti. While the other fish dreamt of flying, Bubbles still lay awake.
Something was missing in his life.
Someone.

While he lay awake, Stormy swam up to him.
"Can't you sleep either?" asked Bubbles.
But his friend Stormy looked scary tonight, and his large gold tooth shone brightly in the moonlight.
He flashed it in front of Bubbles.
"You embarrassed me in front of everyone!" he said.

"I am sorry," apologised Bubbles. But he couldn't even remember what for.

"I am not a vegetarian anymore!" said the shark. He didn't behave like a good friend.

Bubbles swam hastily to the surface to escape, but Stormy blocked his way.

"Let me through!" yelled Bubbles.

At that moment, Reema came to his rescue!

She dived into the pond, and pushed Stormy away with her shining horn! She grabbed Bubbles and lifted him out of the water. He was shaking with fear.
But he finally remembered flying with Reema and felt much better.
“Everything is okay now,” said Reema, touching his scales with her soft nose.

Reema finally sorted out the pond. She took the sharks back to the ocean, where they had enough space. She airlifted the octopus, the jellyfish and Walter, the walrus, back into the shallow sea waters near the coast.

Afterwards, the pond felt lovely and big.

"I should have helped a long time ago," apologised Reema, and rubbed her horn against Bubbles's button nose.

He was very thankful for such a brilliant friend.

Unicorn Stories

The Rainbow Unicorn Visits the Little Boy

Jan Rylewicz

Om KIDZ
An imprint of Om Books International

One night, little Luca had a dream.
A beautiful white unicorn with a spiral horn and flapping wings knocked at his bedroom window.
“Where are you from?” asked Luca.
“I slid down from the rainbow,” said Megan, the unicorn.
“Wow,” he replied, admiring the colourful rainbow overhead.
He had never seen such a beautiful unicorn before.

"Tomorrow the whole world will lose its colour," warned the unicorn. Luca was a little scared.

"I like my colours, especially my red football shirt, my green apple and the yellow flowers in our garden." Unicorn Megan rested on his bed. She liked his fluffy pillows. She neighed gently.

"You will have to go and find the 'Apple of Colour', which will make everything bright and fun again."

"Where do I find the 'Apple of Colour'?" Luca asked.
But Megan had already flown out of his bedroom window and back up the rainbow.
"Goodbye Megan, see you tomorrow!" he shouted, but she did not hear him.
He hoped that he would meet her again because he would not know where to find the magic apple without her.

The next morning, everything was black and white and boring. Black and white toast for breakfast, and white apple juice! Mother's pretty red hair was white like that of Luca's grandmother.
At least Scratchy, his black cat, had not changed. She would always be black!
"Why is my blue work shirt black?" asked dad, looking pasty.
"There is probably something wrong with the washing machine," explained mum.

Outside, everything was grey. Garden and daffodils, snail and butterfly, the apple and the pear tree. Nothing had kept its colour. The roads were grey, as usual. The sun shone greyly in a black sky! Luca saw Megan by the forest. He started running.

She was drinking water from a pond, underneath a tall, pale tree.
"Thank God, you still have your colour," shouted Luca. Amongst all the grey leaves, unicorn Megan sparkled like a diamond.
Her mane was the colour of rainbows.
Her eyes shone like green gemstones.
Her tail was long and fluffy.
Unicorns never lose their colour.
Even when the '100-Year Greyness' strikes.

The 100-Year Greyness is an illness that comes over the forest and city every 100 years. All colours fade and the world looks completely dull.

"Let's save the world," roared Luca.

Megan neighed and blew sparkles from her nostrils.

"We don't have much time."

Wherever Megan put her hooves down, colour returned to the ground.

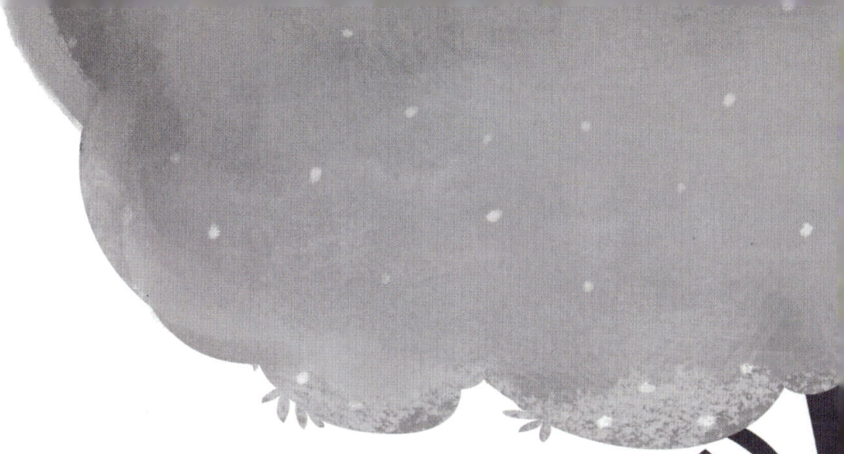

A black conker turned brown. A grey maple leaf, green. Dark flower petals became violet. Megan was a very special unicorn. “Climb on my back and let’s fly. Otherwise we will be too late,” she called, and Luca jumped on her back. He was excited. He had never flown on a unicorn before.

Megan flapped her wings, buzzing like a butterfly. She began rising over treetops, in which parrots and monkeys played chase. Luca wanted to stop and play with them. He liked the way the monkeys screamed. Yet, everyone was colourless.
"Parrots without colours are no fun!" he said. "Let's fly faster and save the world!" neighed Megan.

Megan landed gently. Her flapping wings ruffled the leaves on the trees, like the touch-down of a helicopter.
"The 'Apple of Colour' is guarded by a giant grey squirrel," she explained. "Go and get it back! I will wait here for you."
"Why did he steal the apple?" asked Luca.
"Because he is jealous of all colours."

Luca wished for golden fish in a blue river and for a yellow sun in the sky. He had to find the mean, grey squirrel.

He reached a row of thorny bushes. He didn't want to be pricked. Inside the bushes, it was dark as night.

Right in front of him sat the giant grey squirrel, round and tall as a tree with a long bushy tail.

Hidden under its paws was the brilliant red 'Apple of Colour'. It shone like a crimson jewel.
"Why are you doing this?" asked Luca without fear.
"Because I am jealous of the pretty fur of brown squirrels," he explained. He didn't seem mean anymore.
"But I like your grey fur. I think it's just lovely. Can I touch it?"
The giant squirrel was so happy that he dropped the magic apple. Right at that moment, Luca grabbed it and ran as fast as he could.

Megan was already waiting with her wings buzzing. Luca hopped back on.
"Well done," she congratulated. "You said something kind to him. Kindness always heals the '100-Year Greyness'."
The squirrel started chasing the two friends, but Megan flew faster than a helicopter and a rocket and even lightning. Luca had to hold on tight!

As they flew through the air, the sky turned blue again. Luca stretched out his hand with the apple and touched the sun. It turned bright yellow and started smiling.

They flew close to the tree roofs, so that the leaves turned green again. Luca was very happy.

Like a priest, he blessed the world with his magic apple. Daffodils in gardens turned yellow, bluebells blue, and the violets purple.
Even dad's work shirt was blue as it should be.
"The washing machine seems to be working again," said dad and clapped his hands.
Luca was happy, but sad to say goodbye to Megan, who flew away. He hoped for many more adventures with her.

Unicorn Stories

The Unicorn's Shoes

Jan Rylewicz

Om KIDZ
An imprint of Om Books International

Horses are better. Izzy knew that. From the day she had flown over the stables and watched the horses gallop carefree across the hillsides, she was hooked.

To be a horse, and not a unicorn, wouldn't that be wonderful?

"Unicorns always have to be special, and that is so exhausting," she complained to Tara, her best friend.

"It's not just this being-special-business. It is the way we look. Horses have lovely tails, like the strands of girl hair. What do we have? Oh, I hate my tail so much!"

Tara shook her head, and her horn twisted like a croissant coming out of a baker's oven. She was a proud unicorn!

“I have to go now. I have to be home to discuss the special rank of unicorns in the universe with my parents. How I love those conversations!” Tara could be so lovely, but also extremely annoying. The worst thing about being a creature with magical powers were the feet.

Looking down at them, Izzy blushed.
She was the only unicorn known to do that.
Once, she cried salty tears.
Had anyone ever heard of a crying unicorn?
"What's up, Izzy?" Tara asked.
"The usual. My awful cloven goat hooves! Why can't they be prettier like horses' shoes? I hate my feet so much!"

Tara didn't understand Izzy. Tara loved herself, every pearly inch of her starlight-skin. Her power to teleport from one astral region to the next. And to heal with the touch of her horn!

Unicorns were not allowed to be sad like Izzy. Or were they? Meanwhile, Izzy kept dreaming about the perfect feet.
"Mum, I hate it when my ugly hooves stick up in the air for everyone to laugh at!"

Dad stood high on his hind-hooves, stomping and steaming.
"I've had it up to here, Izzy,"
he snorted, "you should be proud of your hooves and proud of who you are. We are magical unicorns!"

But Izzy was stubborn.
"I will buy myself new shoes!" She declared and flew away. Now she finally knew what she had to do and smiled!

The Thunder and Lightning Dance by the enchanted pond was just around the corner. Izzy was going to surprise everyone with her brand-new feet! "Come. Tara, let's go shopping," she said, dragging her friend away from mirror hour – her favourite time of admiring her beauty in the reflection.
"Where are we going?" Tara asked, not quite done loving herself.
"Shoe-shopping, where else, silly!"

There was only one shop in the whole forest. It was mainly for bears to buy honey, and bees selling it.
Izzy hoped they had a shoe-section!
“How will you pay? Unicorns don’t have money!” Tara said.
“I will pay in honeysuckle, which I collected,” Izzy said and smiled.
Mr Grizzly, the sales consultant in tuxedo, shuffled over to them, squinting hard at the unicorn girls.

“Ma’ams, I believed you were the stuff of legend. It is an honour to have you here as our distinguished guests. Tea or coffee? Juice?”

“No. Thank you,” Tara replied, snootily, “unicorns only drink divine nectar.” Izzy said, “I only want a pair of prety of pretty shoes.”

“Sure thing, two bubbling lemon-topped mango nectars coming right up! With straws, naturally.”

Mr Grizzly whistled, and a badger in blue jeans and pink top appeared behind a set of curtains.

"Wilfried, our finest nectar for these unicorns, please. And bring out our latest collection of the fine Italian shining footwear."

Being a unicorn was not always a bad thing, Izzy thought. It was like being a pop star.

"See, we are sensations!" Tara said, hugging and tapping her best friend with her wings.

It was the day of the big dance. Tara spent most of it glued to her dewdrop mirror, preparing to dazzle everyone at the party with her beauty. "I am fabulous and luxurious!" she sang, flinging herself down from the cloud cushions towards the green forest floor.

Some unicorns were on weather duty.
It was their job to light up the dancefloor with lightning, and summon the thunder soundtrack. Fresh ponds and lakes were whisked up, and the unicorn girls gathered around them, laughing, neighing, falling in love with their wind-rippled reflections. The ponds shone violet like heather, and the lakes like golden starlight juice.

Izzy had always tried to blend in. She never dared to stand out loud and proud. But why should she care about what anyone thought? It was her time to shine!

She slowly flew down from her cloud home. She looked lovely in her cool new footwear and her tail full of glitter. Tara almost didn't recognise her! Izzy was the first on the moonlit dancefloor.

It was too simple and too much fun!

"Come on, shake your legs…I mean, hooves!" Izzy chirped, shaking and grooving to the thunder beats.

The other unicorn girls looked up and admired her. How brave she was!
All unicorns admired marvellous Izzy and her fancy starlight boots. The leather sparkled more brightly than the stars.
"Come on, Tara!" she neighed.
Her best friend trotted over and waved her tail to the music. The two unicorn girls had so much fun that night!

Unicorn Stories

The Flying Unicorn Races with the Eagle

Jan Rylewicz

Om KIDZ
An imprint of Om Books International

Dazzle, the unicorn, loved adventures. She flew elegantly and fast with her unicorn friends in the skies. They played all day long in the mystical Fantasy Forest. When she looked down from high above, she could see the lush green Earth full of beautiful flowers, trees, and strange moving creatures, who seemed to be having a lot of fun!

Dazzle wanted to find new friends on Earth. One day, she flew near the fields close to the earthlings. Dazzle hid behind a tall tree and watched the children kick a small object around. They seemed to be having a jolly good time! Unknown to Dazzle, a hungry bald eagle called Marcus was sizing her up from the sky above.

As he swooped down towards Dazzle, a soccer ball came flying out of the blue and hit him on his head.
Joey, one of the children playing on the field below, had kicked the ball high up.
Marcus the eagle let out an angry squawk, and stopped in its flight, momentarily.

Now Dazzle looked up and saw Marcus. His head gleamed white in contrast to his chocolate-brown body and wings, his eyes were sharp and piercing. Dazzle was frightened. She flew off in the other direction. One of the children,Macy, who was watching Dazzle and Marcus, shouted, “Leave the unicorn alone.” But Marcus was in a naughty mood.

Dazzle needed to rest. But the scary bird was getting closer. "I have to find a way to hide." Yet, a beautiful unicorn with flowing purple-coloured hair and shiny yellow horn on her forehead, could not hide that easily.

She had an idea. Maybe the children could help her hide. She landed gently among them. They all stared at her in awe. Dazzle yelled, "Help me hide from that horrid eagle!"

Courtney asked Macy, "Is the unicorn actually talking to us?" But Macy knew there was no time for surprise. Dazzle needed help now, before the eagle swooped down on her!

She jumped on the unicorn's back and up they went with the eagle in pursuit. Luckily, trees with widespread branches and leaves protected Macy and Dazzle. But Marcus didn't give up easily!

"Don't worry, I have a plan," said Macy, smiling at her fabulous friend. "Let's hide in a cave by the lake."

Macy said confidently, "I will get off and stand next to the cave. You will gallop around the lake then dash into the cave. I will close the entrance with a big stone. The eagle won't be able to see you and fly off."

Marcus had been following Dazzle closely. But he was confused when he saw the small girl by the lake alone. The plan worked! One moment he could see Dazzle, then suddenly, not anymore! Now Dazzle and Macy were safely hidden in the dark cave.

"Time to give up," he grunted,
flying away. Inside the cave the unicorn said, "My name is Dazzle. Thank you for saving my life. I will come back to play with you and your friends." Macy was happy to have a new best friend. She pushed the stone from the entrance and checked that Marcus had gone. It was safe to come out.

Macy watched Dazzle fly off into the evening sky. She admired her beautiful rainbow mane and flapping white wings. Suddenly, Dazzle was on the edge. She spied Marcus far away in the sky, hiding behind a fluffy cloud. She did not want to get into a fight with Marcus.

Lost in thoughts, Dazzle suddenly felt a breath of hot air on her mane. Marcus was almost on her. The bully wanted to play more mean games with Dazzle to scare her. “Did you think you could escape me so easily,” Marcus scoffed. He pulled Dazzle’s beautiful mane.

But all was not lost. Out of the clouds flew Dazzle's mother and father, followed by her unicorn friends. They surrounded Marcus. "Go away, Marcus, you bullying brat," they shouted together. Marcus let go of Dazzle's mane and in his confusion crashed into a towering top of a tree and tumbled, in a mass of ruffled feathers and wings. Marcus had learnt his lesson.

Now Dazzle was finally free! She was happy to be surrounded by her parents and friends. She could hardly believe her eyes!

Dazzle's mother Glitter explained, "Your friends could not find you in Fantasy Forest and were worried. Dolly said you wanted to make friends with human beings! So, we decided to fly down to Earth to find you."

Dazzle smiled, "Thank you all for rescuing me! But I must tell you that the humans are not bad. In fact, a lovely girl called Macy saved my life!" "You better take us with you when you decide to visit the good humans again!" Dolly said with a smile. Dazzle laughed. From now on she often played with the children.

Unicorn Stories

The Singing Unicorn

Jan Rylewicz

Om KIDZ
An imprint of Om Books International

The sky opera stood in the clouds above the mountains.
It showed unicorn dances, unicorn cinema and unicorn sports like horn-locking and eyelash-fluttering.
But it was mainly used for sky operas.
Only unicorns were allowed in it.
Madame Anya was the diva at the opera, singing almost every night.

“La la la la la,” she neighed, so shrill that the moon and the sun moved out of position.
All the unicorns applauded with clacking hooves. Another great performance!
One day, the unicorn singer, Calypso, challenged Madame Anya. Calypso and her daughter Gal were from the poor part of the forest.
Gal wanted her mother to win the first prize. The family badly needed money for food.

The night of the singing duel in the sky opera had come.
"I brought popcorn!" said Godfrey, Gal's younger brother. But as he said it, half of the packet spilled into his lap. "Oh, no!"
"Are you nervous, mother?" asked Gal.
Her mother had never looked prettier. She had even highlighted her hair, of the colour of the evening stars.
"Unicorns don't get nervous!" she lied.

Madame Anya stepped on the stage.
She wore a silken throw and a diamond tiara.
The crowd cheered.
She opened the competition.
She sang, as if opening her mouth for a doctor.
"What is she doing now?" asked Godfrey.
"She is tuning," explained Gal.

Madame Anya's mouth was open so wide that stars bounced from it, sparkling in the night sky. Every high note turned into a baby star, and every low one into a purple planet. At the end of her performance, the night sky was full of new lights. The wild applause lasted almost all night.

But Madame Anya was jealous. She did not want her challenger to win!

Calypso came on the stage, and Gal cheered loudly. Only tired Godfrey had fallen asleep. Calypso opened her mouth, and raised her horn to the stars. She began to sing beautifully.

"IIIIIIIIIIIIIIIIIIIIIIIIIIIIIIIIIIIIII
WIIIIIIIIIIILLLLLLLLLLLLLLLLLL
ALWAAAAAAAAAAAAAAAAYS
LOOOVE...."

But, a jealous Madame Anya secretly tripped her up. And nobody saw her do it!

Calypso fell through the cracks in the clouds and sailed through the sky, landing roughly on the top of a willow tree.
She was injured, and was not able to sing again.
Gal was very sad.
"How will we make money? What will we eat?" she worried.

One day, Gal read the following headline in the newspaper:
PALACE PALLADIUM OPENS DOORS TO STUDENTS.
It was a new singing school, and the main teacher was Madame Anya.
Gal was angry. She decided to sing at the new school and to get the diva arrested!
Gal and Godfrey ate the same meal every day.
Cold stinging nettles for breakfast, and steamed stinging nettles for lunch and dinner.
Something had to change.

The next morning, Gal set out before the break of dawn. As she flew deeper into the forest, she met other animals, who wanted to sing at the Palace Palladium.

There was Mayhem, the monkey, who was good at rapping.

Lotus, the Japanese salamander, who was good on the recorder.

There was the locust brass section, a mini orchestra from Africa.
Freddy Flea, a microscopic singer, yet a superstar amongst the little people.
Benji, the elephant, a master on the trombone, who could carry a dog or a cat on the air he blew out of his trunk.
Hector, the lion, was a rock drummer with a big beard.

When they reached the brand new school, the animals were nervous. They were scratching their heads and shaking their hooves, stinging with their stingers and striking with their tails. Not a single one of them stood still.

Angry Madame Anya opened the balcony windows and shouted:

“Stop fidgeting. Anyone who doesn’t stand still in ten seconds is disqualified!”

Freddy, the flea, was the first contestant. Yet he was so small that Madame Anya didn't even hear him!

He was sad when he left the hall.

Next up was Hector, the lion, who beat his drums hard like thunder with his paws and tail.

"Far too loud!" complained the diva and kicked him out. Hector looked angry.

Now it was Mayhem monkey's turn.
He cleared his throat and got ready to rap.
But he couldn't.
What if she didn't like rap?
"What is it?" asked the impatient diva.
"Just a second," screeched Mayhem.
"Get out. There is no room in this school for stage fright!" yelled the ugly diva, and kicked Mayhem out.
Gal gave him a big hug.
"Don't worry, it will all be fine," she said.

Gal stormed into the hall. Madame Anya leaned lazily on a cushion, drinking sweet unicorn chocolate milk.

"You pushed my mother down the sky opera because you knew she was a better singer than you!"

Madame Anya laughed loudly.

"Of course! I pushed her! I am the only unicorn superstar. Nobody is allowed to challenge me."

But clever Gal recorded the diva's confession.Soon, the unicorn police arrived to arrest her.

By now, Calypso had recovered from her fall. She became the new singing teacher at the Palace Palladium. Everyone loved her. Gal often sang duets with her mother. Now, the family had enough food and money to live. Mayhem monkey passed all his rap exams and made everyone proud.

Unicorn Stories

The Unicorn Goes to School

Jan Rylewicz

Om KIDZ
An imprint of Om Books International

Carmen, the pretty, pink-haired unicorn, was excited. It was her first day at school! "You are the first unicorn ever to go to school!" said Angela, her mother with white hair.

"Come to the garage, I have a present for you," said Peer, her father. He showed her a brand-new red bicycle.
"Wow!" said Carmen, jumping up and down.

Carmen pushed her bike through the forest.
It was too dangerous to ride here.
Many other animals joined her.
They all looked different and interesting!
“Hi, I’m Amelie, the snow leopard,” said
Amelie, a cute little leopard, with
dotty fur.
“I roll around in the snow all day.”
“That sounds like fun!” said Carmen.

"Hello, I am Dave, the giraffe," said a very curious animal with a slender neck. "Could you bend down please so that we can hear you?" asked Carmen politely. "I love chewing tree leaves," he explained, with a mouth full of leaves. A very strong ape sprinting on all fours raced past them, whirling up dust.
"You better hurry up, Mr Grunt doesn't like late students!" thundered Gordon Gorilla.

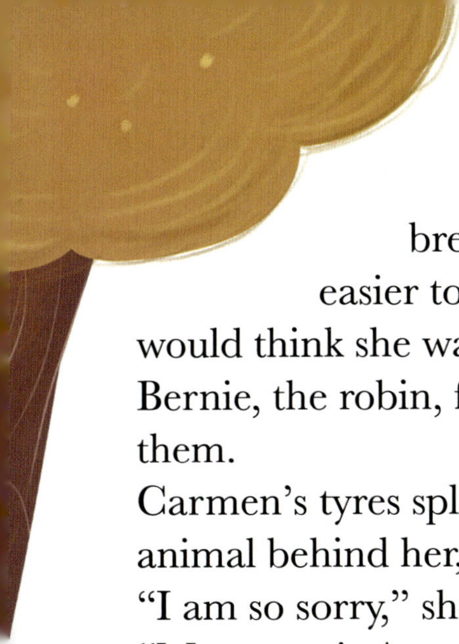

Carmen pedalled faster. She was out of breath! It would have been easier to fly, but then everyone would think she was arrogant.

Bernie, the robin, flew laughingly above them.

Carmen's tyres splashed mud onto a green animal behind her, crawling on all fours.

"I am so sorry," she said.

"My name is Aaron Alligator and I love bathing in mud. Thank you very much for that surprise mud splash party!"

"See you at school, slowcoaches!" teased the alligator, overtaking Amelie and Carmen. By accident, his sharp upper teeth ripped a hole into her back tyre!

"Oh no!" she shouted. All air fizzled out of the tyre.

Dave, the giraffe, was already at the school gate. So was everyone else! Even her new friend Amelie left her behind.

She didn't want to be late either.

If only her father Peer had taught her how to fix a bike.

"Don't you use your magic!" mother had warned.

Using magic was unfair because other animals didn't have it.

Carmen's heart pounded fast. She didn't want to make a bad impression!

She touched the broken tyre with her horn, so that the sunlight could flow into it and make it big.

"BANG!" it sounded, and the tyre exploded. Bits of rubber whizzed all around her.

Oh no, if only she had listened to her wise mother!
She was an hour late for school.
She carefully pushed the door open and glanced into the classroom.
All her friends were sitting at small wooden desks, reading quietly from their books.
At the front of the room stood a heavy, animal.
A pair of reading glasses perched on his very large nose.
It was her teacher Mr Grunt, the hippopotamus.

"Well, who are you then?" he asked.
"I am Carmen, the unicorn."
"Are you late because unicorns deserve special treatment?"
"No," protested Carmen, "I have a lot to learn."
"Then you are in the right place."
Carmen sat down next to a very cheerful chimp.
His name was Ham. He wanted to be an astronaut! Carmen liked Ham straight away.

At lunchtime, the animals stormed around the cafeteria. An elephant balanced a tray of fish and chips on his trunk.
A mouse with a baseball cap grabbed a bit of cheese and chewed with the rodent gang.
Ham, the chimp, juggled bananas, as if he were in a circus. Everyone clapped.
It was like a circus in here. It was brilliant!

"Everyone quiet, and Ham...time-out!" called Mrs Stern, the dinner lady.
"Why is she so thin?" asked Carmen, trying to find somewhere to sit.

"She is only allowed to watch others eat!" explained Amelie. "How sad," said Carmen. She offered Mrs Stern her apple.
The dinner lady smiled brightly.
Helping out and being kind were always good things.

Soon all animals in Mr Grunt's baby class presented their projects.
"Me first!" screamed Ham, jumping up and down.
He banged his wooden desk so that a pile of books flew up and down, up and down.
"Alright, you're up," said Mr Grunt.
Ham held up a cardboard model of the spaceship he had made.
It had a rocket and a landing capsule.
"I will be the world's first chimpo-naut," explained Ham proudly. But Ham was a cheeky chimp. He lit the space rocket!

"Ten, nine, eight, seven, six, five..." he counted.
"What?" said Mr Grunt, who couldn't believe his ears. At zero, the rocket made a terrible hissing noise, like a balloon pumping out air. It began zigzagging and speeding around the classroom.
It zoomed sharply over Carmen's head, and even the small mouse had to duck.
VROOM! It caught fire.

Baby elephant Bruno blasted water from his trunk towards the space craft, but he missed.

He splashed Mr Grunt, so that his glasses fell on the floor! Ham clapped his hands, screaming and hopping from table to table, pushing pens and rubbers and rulers onto the floor.

"I have to help," decided Carmen, "this fire is dangerous."

She flapped her pretty wings next to Ham's crazy, burning spaceship.

With her cute horn, Carmen pushed open a window.
She made it rain in the classroom using her magic.
Sometimes, unicorn magic was the best solution! The heavy rain put out the burning cardboard spacecraft, which dropped to the floor. Ham stopped cheering. Other animals quickly put their raincoats on.
"I love the rain!" sang Aaron the alligator, catching drops with his open jaws.
Everyone was grateful for Carmen's brilliant magic!

Next, Amelie talked about the tall mountains and the white snow which sometimes turned her fur white. All the animals laughed.
"My mother's hair is white, too!"
added Carmen.
When it was her turn, Carmen showed the class how to repair a flat bicycle tyre without using magic.
Everyone was very impressed. A unicorn bike mechanic, wow!